Brave Donatella
and the
Jasmine Thief

Caroline McAlister

ILLUSTRATED BY Donald Hendricks

ini Charlesbridge

Duke Cosimo de' Medici was the richest, most powerful man in Florence. He loved beautiful things: marble statues, crystal vases, cameos carved from onyx, and portraits of himself (after all, he was very handsome).

But most of all, Cosimo loved collecting exotic flowers and trees. Explorers brought him new plants from all over the world. His favorite came from the famous adventurer Vasco da Gama: jasmine, all the way from India.

Cosimo was enchanted by the plant's delicate white flowers and dark, slender vine. But it was the fragrance of jasmine that made it special. It smelled like all the spices of India mingled together: cinnamon, ginger, cloves, and orange peel.

Cosimo planted his jasmine in the Boboli Gardens behind the Pitti Palace, where it flourished. But this was a problem. The jasmine was too easy to grow. What if a servant stole a sprig to grow in his own garden? Then it would become ordinary. Cosimo could not abide ordinary.

Cosimo guarded his jasmine jealously. He forbade his gardeners to remove even one leaf. No one dared disobey one of Cosimo's orders. He was known for tossing his enemies into a dungeon, dumping them into the swift currents of the Arno, or dispatching them himself with a poisoned dagger. He was a very dangerous man.

Cosimo's youngest gardener, Antonio, was in love with a girl named Donatella. He loved the way she walked— determined and purposeful, but graceful. He loved her laugh, with its joyful and playful tone. He loved the smells that came from her kitchen, rich and spicy. They wanted to marry, yet Antonio had no money for a ring and no money to set up house. Made bold by love, he dared to clip a small sprig of the jasmine and hide it under his jacket. Why should Duke Cosimo be the only person in Italy to enjoy this spicy scent?

Antonio presented the sprig of jasmine to Donatella.
"I do not have a gold ring or a silver bracelet to give you,"
he said, "but let this flower show how much I love you.
I have risked my life to bring it to you."

Donatella inhaled the scent of cinnamon, ginger, cloves,
and orange peel. Antonio's action was foolish, but she
knew his words and his heart were true. "I love this flower
more than ten rings," she said, "and I love you more than
all the riches in the world."

Donatella's mother sighed. "You cannot live on fragrance alone. You must have food to eat and a roof over your heads. How will you set up house with a flower? And what will you do if the duke discovers a sprig of jasmine is missing?"

"Don't worry, Mother," said Donatella. "A man with so many grand things could hardly miss something so small."

The next day the duke was in his garden. Turning to admire a new statue, Cosimo noticed a branch missing from his favorite vine. White sap trickled from the place where a spray of flowers had grown just the day before.

In a fury, Cosimo lined up the gardeners, the cooks, the laundresses, the seamstresses, the housemaids, the couriers, the doormen, the servants, and even the coachmen. "Who has stolen my jasmine?" he roared. "I will torture every one of you with red-hot pincers until you tell me."

The housemaids began to sniffle. "It was Antonio," said one of them.

Cosimo arrested Antonio on the spot. "I would kill you myself," he said, "but your blood is too base. It would tarnish my spear." His guards took Antonio to the distant town of Volterra. There Cosimo kept anyone who had disobeyed him in a deep, dark dungeon underneath a tall, narrow watchtower.

When she heard the news, Donatella's mother put her hands on her broad hips. "What did I tell you?" she said.

But Donatella did not cry. Smart as she was, she knew that tears would not free Antonio. She only said, "I know what to do."

She took the sprig of jasmine and planted it in a clay pot. She hid the pot in a back window, where it would get light but could not be seen by curious neighbors. Then she set off for Volterra.

Donatella walked for three days and
two nights to reach the walls of Volterra.

"Even Cosimo's guards must need to eat," she reminded herself. At the back door of the tower, she inquired if they needed help in the kitchen.

When the guards laughed, their spears rattled against their armor. "You cook for us? Look at you. Your clothes are dirty, your shoes are tattered, and it doesn't look as if you're all that well fed yourself."

Donatella smiled. "Excuse my appearance. I have had a long journey. If you will let me clean up, I can cook you sausage and fennel. I can make pasta, too: farfalle and fusilli, gemelli and gigli, radiatore and rotini, cavatelli and conchiglie. Whatever you are hungry for."

The guards' mouths began to water. They agreed to take her on as a cook on a trial basis.

The first night she cooked sausage spiced with fennel.
The next night she baked buns covered with tiny sesame
seeds. Then she made farfalle coated with nuts, oil, garlic,
and fresh basil leaves. The garlic and basil made the guards
thirsty. "Girl!" they yelled. "Make us a drink."

Donatella brought up hot tea infused with the purple
petals of poppies. She had seen bees grow drowsy collecting
nectar from the poppies that grew near the town walls.

When she heard the clatter of their spears dropping to
the ground, then silence, Donatella knew the guards had
fallen asleep. The keys to the dungeon rested on the table
under the hand of one of the guards. Carefully she pried
them from his fat fingers and began her descent into
the dungeon.

She walked down, down, down the cold and slimy stairs. She worried that her footfalls would wake the guards, but they slept on, woozy from the poppies. Donatella was all alone.

At the bottom of the dungeon, she found Antonio sitting on a damp mattress, dirty and disheveled, his head in his hands.

"Quick," she said. "We must go, before the duke's guards wake up."

Antonio looked up in amazement. "What are you doing here? Don't you know that you are risking your life? If the duke finds you have been here, he will kill you."

"You risked your life to bring me the sprig of jasmine," said Donatella. "Now it is my turn."

Antonio stumbled after her up the dungeon stairs. He had known Donatella was beautiful and clever, but he had not known that she was also brave.

When the guards woke up, they saw the door to the
dungeon wide open and realized they had been fooled.
Rather than face the wrath of Cosimo, they fled in four
directions, leaving their spears where they had dropped
them the night before.

There was no possibility of Antonio and Donatella ever returning to Florence. Duke Cosimo had spies and watchmen everywhere in the city. All had orders to kill the jasmine thief and his girlfriend on the spot. "I should have done it myself when I had the chance," Cosimo said as he sniffed the blossoms of his favorite plant.

The one person who knew their whereabouts was Donatella's mother. When soldiers had come and searched her house, she had kept the jasmine safely hidden. Now, under cover of nightfall, she left to join them, the pot of jasmine hidden in her bag. Antonio was a skilled gardener, and the jasmine thrived. They sold it in marketplaces up and down Italy, and soon earned enough money to get married and buy a small house.

To celebrate their good fortune, Donatella wore a sprig of jasmine on her wedding dress.

Her mother smiled. "I was wrong," she said. "You two have managed to set up house with a flower. What could be more beautiful?"

And ever since, it has been the custom in Italy for brides to wear jasmine for happiness and good luck. And while anyone may now grow jasmine, it is not the least bit ordinary. How could it be, when it smells like all the spices of India gathered together: cinnamon, ginger, cloves, and orange peel?

Author's Note

During the 1400s and 1500s, Italy was not a unified country but a collection of city-states. Florence, located on the Arno River in the central region of Tuscany, was one of the richest and most powerful of the city-states. The Medicis, a wealthy banking family, rose to prominence in Florence at the end of the fourteenth century and ruled there for four hundred years.

The Medicis were great patrons of the arts. Some of the most famous artists of the age—Donatello, Botticelli, Michelangelo, and Leonardo da Vinci—produced works of art for the Medicis. Despite their love of the finer things, the Medicis could be brutal in their quest for wealth and power.

Cosimo de' Medici (1519–1574) became the duke of Florence in 1537. Although he was only seventeen when he came to power, Cosimo proved to be a ruthless and effective political and military leader. As the story suggests, Cosimo was suspicious, haughty, cold, and domineering. Because he ruled by fear, he was always on guard himself. He never left the palace unaccompanied by his bodyguards. He wore a vest of chain mail under his coat and carried a sword, a dagger, and several sharp *stiletti*, or thin, razor-sharp knives. His first act as duke was to punish members of the rival Strozzi family who had conspired against him. Many of those involved in the conspiracy died suspiciously in the dank Volterra prison; those who fled to distant cities were hunted down and killed. Antonio and Donatella had reason to fear being pursued.

Cosimo and his wife, the beautiful and wealthy Eleonora de Toledo, moved from the dark Palazzo Vecchio into the grand Pitti Palace in 1560. The palace was purchased from the Pitti family with Eleonora's money. Cosimo hired the architect Vasari to design additions that almost doubled the palace in size. Of course, such an immense dwelling required a vast staff, and both he and Eleonora were demanding taskmasters. As in the story, their punishment of servants was swift and violent: Cosimo once killed his own manservant with a hunting spear for disobeying an order.

On the hill behind the palace, Cosimo planned and laid out the Boboli Gardens. Full of statues and fountains, they are an outstanding example of Italian Renaissance garden design. The story of how Cosimo jealously guarded his jasmine plants appears in Laura C. Martin's *Garden Flower Folklore*. While the story is mostly legend, Cosimo was interested in botany and medicinal plants: he enlarged the herb garden beside the palace and introduced new rotating crops to Florence, importing some of them from the East.

I used storyteller's liberty to give the young gardener and his girlfriend names and to create the character of the practical, reluctant mother-in-law.

Sources

Brion, Marcel. *The Medici: A Great Florentine Family.* Translated by Giles and Heather Cremonesi. New York: Crown Publishing, 1969.

Hibbert, Christopher. *The House of Medici: Its Rise and Fall.* New York: William Morrow, 1975.

Martin, Laura C. *Garden Flower Folklore.* Chester, CT: The Globe Pequot Press, 1987.

McIntosh, Christopher. *Gardens of the Gods: Myth, Magic and Meaning in Horticulture.* London: I. B. Tauris, 2005.

Ward, Bobby J. *A Contemplation Upon Flowers: Garden Plants in Myth and Literature.* Portland, OR: Timber Press, 1999.

This book is for my father, Floyd McAlister, a gardener extraordinaire who taught me to love plants.

—C. M.

For Bobby, Donn, and Johnny, my three sons.

—D. H.

Published by Charlesbridge
85 Main Street
Watertown, MA 02472
(617) 926-0329
www.charlesbridge.com

Library of Congress Cataloging-in-Publication Data
McAlister, Caroline, 1960-
    Brave Donatella and the jasmine thief / Caroline McAlister ; illustrated by Donald Hendricks.
        p. cm.
    Summary: In sixteenth-century Florence, in what would become Italy, Antonio and Donatella
flee the wrath of Duke Cosimo de Medici from whom Antonio has stolen a sprig of jasmine,
and they use that rare plant to make a fresh start. Includes facts about the duke and Italian
history. Includes bibliographical references.
    ISBN 978-1-57091-729-5 (reinforced for library use)
[1. Jasmine—Fiction. 2. Gardeners—Fiction. 3. Conduct of life—Fiction. 4. Cosimo I,
Grand-Duke of Tuscany, 1519-1574—Fiction. 5. Florence (Italy)—History—16th century—
Fiction. 6. Italy—History—16th century—Fiction.] I. Hendricks, Donald, 1932- ill. II. Title.
PZ7.M478252Br 2010
[Fic]—dc22   2009026647

Printed in China
(hc) 10 9 8 7 6 5 4 3 2 1

Illustrations done in Prismacolor colored pencils and Prismacolor black fine line marker
    on Strathmore white 16-lb. layout bond paper
Display type and text type set in Rennie MacIntosh Renaissance and Centaur MT
Color separations by Chroma Graphics, Singapore
Manufactured by Regent Publishing Services, Hong Kong
Printed February 2010 in ShenZhen, Guangdong, China
Production supervision by Brian G. Walker
Designed by Diane M. Earley